Corbin's Catacombs

James Pack

VaudVil

© 2022 - James Pack
All rights reserved. Printed in the United States of America by VaudVil. An imprint of Pack Enterprises LLC, Tucson, Arizona.

No part of this book may be reproduced or transmitted in any form or by any means, graphic, electronic, or mechanical, including photocopying, recording, taping, or by any information storage retrieval system, without the permission, in writing, from the publisher or author, except in the case of brief, informing quotations embodied within articles or reviews.

ISBN 979-8-9859342-0-5 (print)
ISBN 979-8-9859342-1-2 (ebook)

Poetry Titles by James Pack

Black Chaos
Cats, Coffee, Catharsis
Men are Garbage
Pariah Bound: The Lonesome Poetry

Other Titles by James Pack

The Morbid Museum (Short Stories)
Mushaburui: A Mental Health Journey (Nonfiction)
The Tommy Gun (Novella)

Mademoiselle's Introduction

Bonjour et bienvenue. I am honored to escort you through my beautiful collection within my catacombs. My name is Iphigenia Corbin. You may call me Mademoiselle Corbin. Within these cool, dark chambers are various art pieces from my private collection. My most treasured things I have acquired in my long life.

You see, I am what's called a "Baku." Baku consume the nightmares of mortal creatures. We take them for sustenance, and we take them so people like you are not burdened with them. It is not often that one is appreciated for the work they do. So, I distract myself by collecting and creating art which was inspired by nightmares and other spooky things.

What I will share with you today is but a small fraction of what I've collected. Out of modesty, I will not tell you which is my work or the work of others. Instead, I will let the art speak for itself. I do not wish to influence you in choosing your favorite piece.

Should anything in this ossuary of art cause you discomfort or uneasiness, you are welcome to step away for a moment and rejoin me when you feel ready. There is no shame in needing a short break. I find I need one now and then, and I spend much of my time in this darkness. Darkness was never intended to last forever.

Now, *mes petitis monstres*, let us venture into the world of darkness. A world that can be terrifying, spooky, and most often, *très beau.* Stay close or you may lose yourself. *Allons-y!*

Hellcats

You've heard of hellhounds
Coming for your soul
After a deal with
A crossroads demon
But a hellcat needs
No reason to kill
Born of hellfire
Without a master
And demons will run
When hellcats roam free
Not even the hounds
Pick fights with the beasts
The devil's fire
Can't tame the hellcats

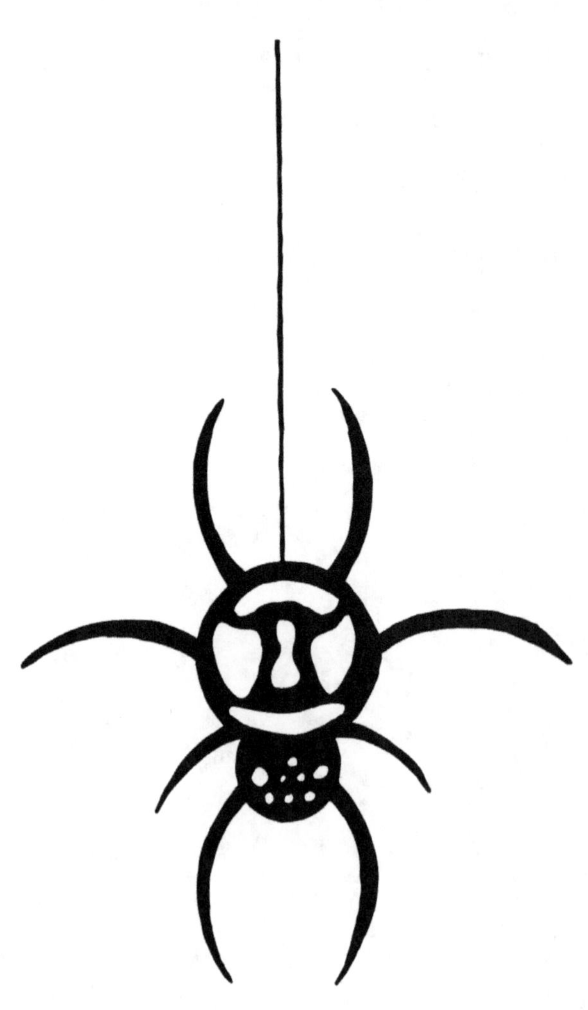

"Spider, Spider"
Sharpie on paper
Private Collection

Cobwebs and Caskets

Spider spider
Spinning your web
Catching insects
At a low ebb
Enswathing food
Setting your traps
Digesting bugs
That you have wrapped
Eaten alive
Gruesome some say
Your way of life
Scares them away
Spider spider
Cunning hunter
Misunderstood
Spooky crawler
Feast on your prey
Eat your supper
All live in fear
Of the spider

Monster Movies

I am the Wolf Man that howls at the night
This curse that I live with and live to fight
While helpless people run away in fright
My inner demons take control tonight

They call me the Monster made from Madness
My brain is abnormal; full of sadness
I seek out only love and happiness
Rejected I retreat to the darkness

From the depths of the Lagoon I wander
Seeking those who've awoken my slumber
These people have torn my home asunder
Now they will pay greatly for this blunder

They came to my Tomb for riches and fame
So, I've brought upon them curses and shame
The vengeance I bring shall never be tame
Death and fear will come from the Mummy's name

Swathed in bandages and dark spectacles
Using a new drug so unpractical
Able to render one invisible
This power makes me so unstoppable

Together good and evil live inside
Two have become one and Jekyll and Hyde
The madness that conquers the mind with Pride
Immoral acts you can no longer hide

I'm the Countess who rises from the grave
Seeking a love as my eternal slave
Draining the red life from those that I crave
This sad world no monster or man can save
They all, in the end, will become my slaves

The New Toy

yes, yes everybody knows
what happens to toys and where they all go
they are torn, broken, and beaten
but nobody knows what's the real reason

perhaps they are attacked all of a sudden
but what are the odds of being attacked by somethin'
when a toy is played with far more than often
it will be attacked by those who have been forgotten

he is defiled and harmed
in such a frightening fashion
he is beaten to a pulp
his leg will need to be refastened

the toys are so mean
there are too many to fight
he'll get them somehow
they will all cry in the night

the fire burned everything
the master did not come from the room
if I cannot play with him
then neither can you

"Turnip Lantern"
Sharpie on paper
Private Collection

Hoberdy's Lantern

It was a painful day
When he carved me
He cut a face in me
Scooped my insides
Placing a candle there
And I became
A lantern with a face
He carried me into
The darkest night
Spirits surrounded him
He was ignored
They avoided my face
Lighting the way
I don't know if he could
See the spirits
He created me so
I could see them
When he got home he placed
Me by his door
And the spirits never
Approached his home
That night I was reborn
To keep him safe
He told me to watch for
The one called Jack
And I did until my
Candle went out

A Child's Nightmare

"time for bed"
my mother said
"you have school in the morning"
she tucked me in
kissed me then
crept away silently
I laid there for a bit
and then the feeling hit
something was watching me
I sat up rather quick
turned the light on which lit
my room and I saw nothing
with a sense of relief
I try to go to sleep
but alas I still feel eerie
over to the closet I sneak
and I hear the door creak
then dive back in bed like a swimmer
oh, it's just the cat
"get out of here Matt"
it's calm in my room once again
the closet door flies
and something skulks in
in fear I throw the covers over my head
I hear something breathing
I feel my heart racing
I hope I'm just dreaming again
the blankets get yanked off
in the air I am tossed
I land on the floor and crawl under the bed
something grazed my coat
my heart is in my throat
there's something walking towards me
its feet have claws
which probably slice logs
its skin is slimy and black
I'm screaming in fear
but nobody hears
and the creature tries to grab me
another comes from the side
and another from behind

they drag me back to the closet from which they came
it's dark in this place
can't see my hand on my face
and several monsters are above me
their mouths are wet and slimy
"MOMMY!" I am crying
and like hungry lions they begin to feast

And the Moon Wept

The brick walls in the alley
Bounced the sound around
Echoes –
The bullet was a .357 magnum
It released from a
Double action silver plated
Colt Python Revolver
A custom bullet
Pure silver –
It spiraled through the air
Chased by flames and smoke
Fading into nothing
As the bullet advanced
Glistening with moonlight
The full moon so bright
Illuminating the alley
To look like day –
The beast's breath steamed
From the cold air
Out from its snarling mouth
It turned to see
The silver bullet approach
No time to move –
The bullet spiraled into
Fur and muscle
No pain at first
Then the burning of
Hot metal on skin
The burning radiating out –
As gunshot echoes dispersed
They were followed by
A howl or a scream
The beast fell back
Clutching its furry chest

With a thud –
The fur shrank away
Revealing a pale man
Steam rising from his face
He looked at the blood
On his hand and chest –
He cracked with laughter
The laughs ricocheting
Through the alley
Then it stopped
As fast as it started
The steam evaporated

"Weeping Moon"
Sharpie on paper
Private Collection

13

Vampires

Our lives are drained by the
Shtriga witch
Which has taken the souls
Of immigrant children

It's taken the souls
Black, brown, and yellow
Of immigrant children
No screams or bellows
How Columbia
Palisades the WASPs

These drained soiled bodies
Unwashed
Unwashed

Candy Cravers

trick or treat
trick or treat
I seek something
sweet to eat
some candy
in this bag of mine
as I finish
my little rhyme
if no sweets
are received
than a trick
to you I leave
if it suits you
fine and dandy
but I'm a trickster
that likes my candy

The Evil Tlea of the South Sea

the Sun shone bright upon the sea
it glistened and sparkled with glee
but near twilight it said to me
as I sat in my boat with three
"I bid you goodnight as I leave,
and warn you of the evil Tlea!
A creature of death that is He.
Your demise; by him it will be!"
the Sun's grave warning we did heed
we sat perplexed, what did he mean
while He sank, we heard a strange scream
miles from home, the land of Smeeth
lost in thought of the evil Tlea
our death; by him would surely be

we sailed away on our wee boat
slowly losing all sense of hope
no land to see within my scope
we drifted on, we didn't know
where we were or which way to go
the Moon called to us, "You there, Ho!
To be free, faster you must row.
Those pure of heart will make it home,
if you are not, Hell you will roam!"
another warning, this is so
but we still have not seen our foe
all these cautions but a no show
is this all real, how do we know
Tlea will not keep us from home

a noise rang out across the sea
the Moon had gone, too dark to see
"Who here wishes to pass by me?"
a cold, rough voice called from beneath

"To pass one must first be received,
by the great and all mighty Tlea!"
"Forgive us!", I called out to He
"Did not mean to disturb your sleep!"
"You there the booming one who speaks,
I foresee your future is bleak.
Tonight, your life I'll take from Thee!"
"DO NOT TAKE ME!!", I beg and plead
by morning the boat held just three
thanks to Tlea of the dark South Sea

An Interlude With Mademoiselle

Rebonjour! Are you enjoying things so far, *mes petitis monstres*? I hope so. The one with the werewolf is one of my favorites. Have you chosen a favorite yet? I hope you will see the rest before choosing one. There is still so much to see.

But first I wish to tell you more about my race, the Baku. Some believe Baku are chimeras, creatures whose bodies are made of many different animals. This is true. There are many Baku like this. You might say, "But mademoiselle, you are not like this. You are a beautiful woman." *Oui*, I am quite lovely, no?

You see, most Baku are this animal like creature. And many stay this way their whole lives. A lucky few, like myself, who live long enough and consume enough nightmares can…how do you say…um, change? Evolve? Something like this. The very few of us make up a council of elder Baku. Most of the things we do are very bureaucratic and dull. But I always look forward to our annual banquet.

Sometimes we do have to act against those who would do us harm or harm to the world. Our ultimate nemeses are the Mares. Vicious little creatures who insight nightmares in others and feed off the fear from their prey. I believe mortals call them sleep demons or something like this. They would unmake the world if not for the Baku.

Oh, forgive me, I am rambling. Sometimes I carry myself away. Let's think of things more pleasant. Shall we continue exploring my collection? *Oui, oui!* Come *mes petitis monstres*. There is more for me to show you. *Par ici s'il-vous-plait.*

The Demon Spawn

Born from Hellfire in a blazing rage
He hurts the wicked and all vicious beasts
He has no equal and he never speaks
If you see him it's already too late

He has two fire swords made for power
But he's just as deadly with his bare hands
He captures wicked souls to pass judgement
Some say he does this only for pleasure

You'll never outrun the Demon Spawn
You'll never hide from the Demon Spawn
No one will survive the Demon Spawn
Death awaits all from the Demon Spawn

Everyone fears him even Princes of Hell
He's a hunter of demons and angels
He's the assassin of celestials
He's the only one and nothing kills him

Born from Hellfire in a blazing rage
He has no equal and he never speaks
He captures wicked souls to pass judgement
Everyone fears him even Princes of Hell

"Monster"
Sharpie on paper
Private Collection

The Monster That Ate My Mommy

It didn't eat her right away
The monster that ate my mommy
It lived with her for a long time
Taking a small piece now and then

She never saw it but I did
A smoke creature floating behind
With claws and fangs but made of air
Lurking with shadows and feeding

I warned her – she never listened
I cried when the monster ate her
I thought it would come for me next
It vanished like steam with a grin

I tell people the story of
The monster that ate my mommy
They don't believe in scary things
Some of them have their own monsters

The black smoke waiting to eat them
Will I see mine if I get one
Do I have one eating me now
The same one that ate my mommy

Hunting for Teeth

out hunting for teeth
that will be used no more
from those whose souls do sore

this One is so fresh
just hanged he was this mourn
from flesh his life is torn

maggots start their feast
grotesque though it does seem
tis easier unseen

prying teeth from thee
seems to be so unjust
this won't stop my hard thrust

I beseech my Lord
do not punish me here
his teeth I do not fear

in my own judgment
I intend to reuse
these Pearls are my Muse

Muster for the Massacre

The sheep still scream
Forced from their families
A cacophony of cruelty
When the false shepherds came
The chupacabras organized
This systematic oppression
What does a goat sucker
Fear from a little lamb
Chupacabras care nothing
For the surrendered sheep
Their only plan is to
Feast on the flesh of the flock

Diary of Djinn

take a look in the mirror
and tell me what you see
does the image satisfy
you must reveal to me
how you truly feel inside
when the reflection gleams
is this your one desire
with me we'll make your dreams

I come from another place
a place where magic's real
with the snap of my finger
I can do as you will
be careful what you wish for
I'll rearrange the deal
you'll get what you want and then
the dream will soon be killed

I'm a trickster by nature
a rather good one too
I'll hear your wish word for word
but it still won't come true
with the thought of happiness
I think I'd rather spew
if you give my lamp a rub
Death'll be waiting for you

"Djinn"
Sharpie on paper
Private Collection

The Wraith Riders

through the night we shall ride
seeking imperfection
the purpose of our lives
to commence dissection
with our dark piercing eyes
we see your infection
the shrieking of your cries
will fuel our intentions
our never-ending drive
ensures your destruction

Loki the Clown

laughter, laughter all around
for you see I am a clown
the make-up, the hat, I'm loved by the crowd

the crowd disperses, I exit to my chambers
the creature within now becomes angered
the satisfaction of slaughter shall be savored

you laugh at me now, you laughed at me then
it's your demise that now begins
in my presence all have sinned

A Visit from Stingy Jack

Twas the night of Halloween and around the porch
Candles in pumpkins flickered, a face for a torch
Trick-or-Treaters came in guise as monsters and ghouls
Collecting bags of candy as precious as jewels

We kept the porch light turned on, a sign of safety
This informed those sweet cravers we offered candy
We soon gave out all our treats and turned off the light
Then we readied ourselves to turn in for the night

In the middle of the night I woke for a spell
My body froze still because I could hear a yell
I looked out and saw a man, a lantern in hand
A ghostly figure so thin with a face so bland

"Who are you?" I asked with fear. He said, "Call me Jack."
Shadows dancing on his face, his gaze held me back
He moved it towards the pumpkins then he backed away
"Your protections are working." He said, "I won't stay."

He sauntered off down the street holding out his torch
He stopped at each house to look for an empty porch
They all had pumpkin lanterns and away he walked
A spooky spirit named Jack, what is it he stalks

Jack-o-lanterns protect us from evil spirits
Use a pumpkin lantern for unwelcome visits

"Stingy Jack"
Sharpie on paper
Private Collection

The Chill

as days go by and time stands still
you learn the meaning of that Chill
the one that hits you in bad times
when the bells strike their eerie chimes
the Chill that no man can withstand
its cold edge is by far too grand
the Chill that haunts one in his dreams
feeds off the power from his screams

The Four Horsemen

the scroll is broken
out of the depths comes Conquest
the white horse rides on

with a bow and crown
he will take on the masses
Conquest will ride on

the scroll is broken
out of the depths comes Bloodshed
the red horse rides on

with a sword in hand
she will take on the masses
Bloodshed will ride on

the scroll is broken
out of the depths comes Famine
the black horse rides on

with her scales in hand
she kills and starves the masses
Famine will ride on

the scroll is broken
from the darkest depths comes Death
the pale horse rides on

with Hades behind
he will conquer the masses
they belong to Him

Mademoiselle's Farewell

I'm afraid we have come to the end, *mes petitis monstres*. I hope you have enjoyed the spooky time with me. I know I enjoyed your company and escorting you around my catacombs. It is moments like these I think I should have maybe a gift shop. Then I remember I do not like the 'assle.

Though I do not have these things like souvenirs, I hope the memories from our little crusade…wait, this is not the word. I think adventure is more suitable. I hope the memories from our adventure will stay with you forever.

Perhaps we will have more time on your next visit, and I can tell you more about myself and about we the Baku. If you fear having nightmares, we can come to help with this. Many of us are friendly, but not all of us are as beautiful as *moi*. Do not miscomprehend. The looks, this is not everything. One's spirit and heart, these are important things. And I love you all for coming to visit with me.

But now you must go, I'm sorry to say. Fear not for we shall meet again, *mes petitis monstres*. Don't let your nightmares keep you up at night. *A la prochaine.*

A Letter from the Author

      I hope you enjoyed this collection. This was my first attempt at framing a story around my individual poems. I hope it made for a more interesting read. This was also an opportunity for me to develop a character that I will use in future works. I hope readers have a desire to learn more about Mademoiselle Corbin and her race, the Baku. If you've read this far, I hope you will leave an honest review. I am always interested in what others think of my work, whether it's good or bad.

      I plan to present my poetry in this manner in future books though I may change the fictional character that presents each book. I have many stories and books that are in progress. You can always learn about what's new or coming soon on my website and email newsletter. Thank you for reading and I hope you enjoyed the poetry.

~ James

About the Author

James Pack is a member of the Horror Writers Association and has published several collections of poetry and short fiction. Learn more about James and his collected works on his personal blog www.thejamespack.com. He lives in Tucson, AZ.

www.ingramcontent.com/pod-product-compliance
Lightning Source LLC
Chambersburg PA
CBHW060509300726
48975CB00008B/2713